Everything,
Then and Since

Everything, Then and Since

stories

MICHAEL PARKER

DURHAM, NORTH CAROLINA

Everything, Then and Since

Library of Congress Cataloging-in-Publication Data

Parker, Michael.
Everything, Then and Since / by Michael Parker
p.   cm.
ISBN-13: 978-1-4951-5767-7

This is a work of fiction. No identification with actual persons (living or deceased), places, buildings, and products is intended or should be inferred.

Published in the United States of America

Cover design: Flying Hand Studio
Cover and author photos: Tasha Thomas
Interior design: F. H. Spock & Associates

Published by
BULL CITY PRESS
1217 Odyssey Drive
Durham, NC 27713

www.BullCityPress.com

"We live in a dim inkling or a rapt afterness."

—Rodney Jones

Contents

You Can't Talk, Shake a Bush

WHEN ALL HIS BROTHERS and sisters had started school and he was left alone at home, his mother sometimes let him take walks with an old man who lived in the neighborhood. The boy had no idea how old the man was, though it seemed significant to him that the man, like the boy, stayed home during the day, instead of going to work, like his father, or to school, like his siblings. The man wore suspenders, sometimes walked with a cane, draped wet handkerchiefs around his neck in hot weather. His skin was saggy and stained. The old man spoke in curious phrases that made the boy smile even though he did not understand what the man meant. You can't talk, shake a bush! the old man would say when he came to fetch the boy for walks. The boy was almost always first to the door to greet the old man but sometimes he was playing in the closet under the winter coats when his mother called to him and he would run to the door disappointed, for in front of the boy's mother, the old man would lean down and put his hands on his knees and say things like, Why there he is, there's my number one buddy, are you ready to go exploring? In other words, he would say the sorts of things others would or could have said in a voice older people reserved to talk to kids who were not old enough to go to school.

But when they were away from the house, embarked on their journey, especially on the days when the old man brought the boy his very own walking stick, and they left the hilly streets of their neighborhood to travel up the path beneath the power lines to a patch of blackberry bushes, or took the narrow trail past the playground to the quiet green pond in the woods, the old man would talk to him in the way the boy preferred. Not only would he tease him with his strange sayings, he would tell the boy stories about when he was the boy's age. These stories were filled with trains, mules, swimming holes, pennies, barns, ferries, candles, snow, radios, alleyways, hail, catfish, cousins, school dances, snakes, skates, dogs named Ranger or Scout, bicycles, chalk, fever, newspapers, dams, and many other things about which the boy was equally ignorant and interested. The stories the old man told as they walked slowly up and down the hills of the neighborhood were not like the stories the boy's parents or older siblings read to him at night before bed: words in blocks beneath pictures of mostly children, animals, and forests. The stories the old man told were not in blocks and instead of some space created for a picture, instead of the words *stopping* for pictures, the words *were* pictures, but moving ones, almost like cartoons but not loud or sped up like the cartoons the boy was allowed to watch with his siblings on Saturday mornings. The old man talked and the boy saw him duck as a shoe flew over his head and landed in a pie on the dinner table. The boy smiled at the faces of the grown-ups seated around the table. He forgot he was walking. It was neither hot nor cold out. The old man's no-count uncle ran through the woods pursued by the father of the girl he was courting, who was armed with a shotgun. The old man's uncle came suddenly upon a sawmill. He heard it before he spilled out of the brush into the clearing where black men bent over long, loud saws and a train, loaded with boards, idled on a track at the far edge of the clearing. Let's steal this train, the old man said to the boy, and he stopped suddenly in the middle of the path that led to the quiet pond in the middle of the woods, waiting for the boy to climb with him onto the engine and into the cab and escape on the stolen train, bullets above their head, the trees turning blurry and bleeding eventually into another story.

But it was the story of the train, idling alongside the tracks, ready and waiting, their ticket out of harm's way, that the boy told his parents and his siblings at the dinner table that night. Only he did not tell it as if it had happened to the old man's uncle, because it hadn't, it didn't; it happened to him and to the old man as they were on their way to the quiet green pond in the woods. He saw nothing funny about the story—in fact, it was the opposite of funny—so he did not understand when everyone, even his father, who usually walked in the house right as supper was being laid out on the table and smelled of the paper plant he ran and was too tired to talk, laughed. No one said why they found his story funny; no one said anything to him at all. Since the only difference between everyone else at the table and him was the fact that they had been to school, the boy decided you went to school to learn when to laugh. But the boy already knew what was funny. The funniest thing in the world was when people tried to hide behind objects that did not come close to concealing them. Like once when the old man said they were being followed by the banditos, quick let's hide behind this tree, but the tree he squatted next to was just a sad little sprig that did not come up to the boy's shin. The boy looked around the table and saw his siblings and parents attempting to hide behind shakers of salt and pepper, glasses of iced tea, a bottle of ketchup. At last he joined them in laughter, and because it took him so long to get the joke, they all started laughing again.

Widow's Walk

THE BABYSITTER HAD NEVER SEEN an attic or a basement, since she had lived all her seventeen years in a trailer so close to the Sound that even houses were built up off the ground. One afternoon she put the baby to bed in her crib on the old sun porch, pulled all the blinds and curtains to fool day into night. Sitting just outside the nursery on a long wooden bench, she waited for the child to fall asleep. The bench ran down a corridor almost as wide as the trailer where she lived with her mother and two younger brothers.

When the house was built in the 1840s they kept the hallways wide to allow a good breeze between the front porch and back, the baby's father had told her on the first day of the job. He took her through each room and talked of things like crown molding and wainscoting. He called their walk through the house a *tour*, which reminded her of when she was still in school and they climbed in buses and followed their teacher through the loud rooms of the Dr. Pepper bottling plant. The father called the bench a *pew* and said it had come out of the Episcopal church downtown, which her mother had pointed out to her one day, claiming all the people who worshipped there were stuck-up drunks. The babysitter wondered why anyone would put a church pew in a hallway. It was hard and it hurt her back but she sat there every day during nap-time, listening for the baby (who was not really a baby anymore; she was almost three, but the babysitter had answered an ad for a babysitter and so the baby in her mind was a baby) to stop chastising her stuffed snake. She stared at the carpet, which the mother had once referred to as a *runner*. It seemed to the babysitter that this couple had their own words for everything and that it did not change what the things were, so as soon as they were gone she would take the child into the kitchen and pull things out of the drawers and say to the child, What is this? Spoon, the child would say and the babysitter would say, Damn right, it's just a spoon.

Finally the babysitter heard the light ragged sleep-breath of the baby. The babysitter knew that the child's breathing would always sound alarmingly syncopated because she had had a baby herself, though the baby was taken away from her, a fact that the couple with the huge hallways could never know. Breath rose, and it fell; it stopped and started no matter how much you want for it to be even and regular. Nevertheless, the babysitter wanted it for the baby and she wanted it for herself.

Behind the door at the end of the hallway rose the attic stairs. On warm days not yet hot enough for air conditioning, the door was open to allow a fan to cool the upstairs of the house. On those days she was told to leave the windows in the sun porch open just a few inches so the fan would draw the breeze, but the fluttering curtains terrified the child. She stood up in her crib crying about ghosts and so the babysitter closed the windows and the child soaked the sheets of the crib with sweat and woke cross and the babysitter said to her, Well, which is it? You have to choose. Either you see ghosts or you burn up.

Today the windows were open. There was a breeze. The babysitter had never actually seen the fan, but it sounded monstrous and disturbing, like the loathsome snarling that filtered most days through the woods surrounding the trailer. Chainsaws, backhoes, neighbor boys riding ATVs through the cabbage fields. Even so far from town, machines drowned out the birdsong, the rustle of wind through pine needles that the babysitter remembered hearing when she played in the dirt yard when she was not much older than the sleeping baby.

The fan was off and the door was shut. The child was asleep and would be for an hour at least. The babysitter pushed open the door into a heat that she understood well from living in a treeless field through summers when there was no money to run window units. The sloped roof had nails sticking out of its boards. Pink thick blankets of insulation stretched into corners so faraway dim she wasn't sure the attic had an end. The floor was strewn with suitcases, as if the father, home from a trip, had tossed the bags from the top of the stairs. The babysitter had never owned or even seen inside a suitcase because she had never been on a real trip. Once a boyfriend was taking her to Kings Dominion, her extra clothes and makeup and toothbrush stuffed in a plastic sack, and before they even crossed the Virginia line, he got pulled over for speeding and it turned out his license had been suspended. She had to call her mother to come pick her up from the magistrate's office, but her mother's boyfriend Raymond showed up instead. On the endless ride home he called her boyfriend names and told her how worthless she was.

The babysitter opened a red vinyl suitcase and studied the zippered pouches, the compartments for shoes. She stepped over the suitcases, drawn to the light that spilled in from the double doors. Outside was a tiny balcony with wooden bars. The couple probably had a name for this, too, but it was a balcony to her. Through the towering steeples of town she saw the drawbridge over the intracoastal waterway, raised to let a yacht pass. She was higher than she'd ever been, higher than the pines, a part of the sky, so high she could not be brought down to testify against Raymond and what he did to her, too high to hear her mother claim Raymond was a sweet man who'd had a hard upbringing, how can you say those things about him? Far below she saw her car parked in front of this huge house. Her red Mustang. Ten years old and the back quarter panel was painted with primer and three of the hubcaps were missing but it was the only thing in the world that was hers alone. The sight of it did not make her proud as it once had, but suddenly terrified that it was all she'd ever own, that everything after would have to be shared with the same sort of men her mother brought home, then three weeks or three months later threw out. The babysitter went inside and turned on the fan. It was burning up inside the attic. It took a few seconds for the fan to come to life but when it did it was so loud she knew she would not hear the baby should the baby wake and cry out. She knew she should go down, but she wanted the doom she'd felt to be blown right through her by the breeze sucked from the sky by the fan. At least I won't ever have so many things I have to make up names for them, the babysitter said into the wind, and the fan chopped her words up so that they resembled sleep-breath and sent them down to the baby, who woke to see, through the bars of her crib, the billowing skirts of the woman whose house this once was, come again to swish along the corridor in search of the husband who had never returned from the sea.

Medicine Girl

IN HER LEAVING she was a trail of white flashing in the green at the edge of a pasture. Ragged garment, or wings of some sweet angel? After she soothed your suffering, you could only make out shapes, and all you could hear was the pelt of rain upon frond and leaf as the forest took her in again. I asked you all this morning to tell me what is your favorite sentence, she said to Walter and me, as she went about preparing her gift to us, and only because my veins ached and I wanted what she came to give me I said, A noun is a person, place, or thing. What does that even mean, said Walter beside me in the next bed, his arm gone, his house gone, his wife gone, half his mind gone. In the night he'd wake us all, declaiming the presence of an imaginary erection. He did not like to wait on medicine girl; he only liked it when she came to him first. Okay, she said to me, let's break it down, this sentence of yours. Favorite person? Either Marcus Garvey or Jane Pauley, said Walter, but it wasn't his turn, she wasn't talking to him, I told him so. Walter said, He's going to say something stupid like JFK or LBJ, but medicine girl moved over to tend to him first because she knew I could suffer longer. He held up his arm like he had a question, and I watched him slump into the bunk, float away. Buried at sea, he would call it when he came back. Look at the dragoons I stole from a galleon. Hootie and the Blowfish! Walter deeply in his free dive, she came to me again. I can't think of anyone, I said to her. That you admire? That I remember, I said. From before? At all, ever. Sshhh, she said, as the bell of her sleeve brushed my face, or maybe it was the breeze from the rotating floor fan, or a memory of my mother's hand brushing hair out of my eyes. What about a favorite place? The eaves, I said. Like Christmas and New Year's, she asked? Like the time before the time? No, I said, like in the attic. Where the floor becomes the ceiling. Like where the ocean turns into the sky. Good, she said, that is so good. Scoot over, she said, sitting by me on the bed. Now, just one more. She meant what thing. But things were like people; there aren't any, I said. No things? she asked, as she touched the inside of my elbow with her wand. Nothing, I said, because maybe that's what put me there in the bed next to Walter, maybe that's why I did what I did to myself, and why I lived instead of died. Because I was too scared to admit there were things I still believed in. But her question reminded me. She wasn't supposed to be reminding me. It's just something I saw chalked up on some board, I said, it doesn't mean any one thing, it's just, you asked. Two feet away Walter's air bubbles rose toward the ceiling of the ward and I envied even impotent one-armed Walter. Three times a day she came to us all, Walter and the man next to him whose chest was crushed by a car he climbed up under. She came to the lightning struck, the eat-up-with cancer. Into our arms she delivered her mercy, after which she went where they all went, person, place, thing: into the line of shadow at the edge of pasture, into that narrow mile of mouth, dumping me at the crossroads to wait on the time before the time to come along, pull over, and pick me up.

How to Be a Man

WHEN HE WAS IN HIGH SCHOOL, the boy took a job in the afternoons and on weekends at a drugstore. The alcoholic pharmacist yelled at him for things like being sixteen and not knowing how to back a trailer or put water in a car battery. He could not squeegee the windows worth a damn, and the one time he was allowed to run the register, it came up just shy a dollar. Go clean the items in the window, the pharmacist said to him one afternoon, and the boy took a dust rag to the wheelchairs, canes, walkers and other medical supplies staged on the platform by the plate glass. The arrangement of the items bothered him; he was prone to moving the furniture around in his bedroom every few months so that he could walk into the room and feel like he'd never been in it before, or that it belonged to someone else, someone with vision and options. Once he even took the sliding doors off his closet and pushed the head of his bed against the wall, and he did not even mind when he woke to a nightmare of jungle and vine, only to realize he was being grazed by the cuffs of his Sunday trousers. Lying in bed among belts and neckties hanging from coat hangers made him feel he was living in a city, in an apartment so small he had no choice but to put his bed in a closet, far from his parents and the pharmacist. He wanted to transform the window of the drugstore into something similarly fresh and disorienting, but there wasn't much to work with. It wasn't fully possible to arrange the merchandise in such a way that did not say to people on the street, Not only are you going to die, but we are going to make some money off your demise. But in order to create the opposite emotion he felt when he woke with his head in a closet, he would have to leave everything the way it was, the way it had been since he'd taken this job, probably since the drugstore first opened its doors. And now the boy felt stuck: he did not like the pharmacist and he did not want him to make any money at all, much less profit off of the elderly and infirm, but leaving things the way they were, depriving the world of the spark of renewal, seemed to him equally distasteful. And so, seized with an anxiety that produced in him not jitters but lassitude, he sat down in a wheelchair to try and think what to do. The pharmacist must have been busy or drinking with his buddies in the stockroom, for an hour passed and the boy sat undisturbed in the wheelchair, struggling with the confusion of his desires as outside people passed by without a glance his way. And he hated them for it, and he loved them for it, too.

Recruitment

THAT EVENING she drove deep into the southern end of
the county, where the soil turned sandy and thick and
then disappeared under black water. Swamps stretched to
the ocean, forty miles south. These were the hardest kids
to reach. The bus drive to the high school was forty-five
minutes for those who lived off these backroads. Dirt
roads with clusters of mailboxes, six or seven families
living off a rutted two track in mostly trailers onto which
they had built additions listing on stacked blocks, half-
walled, half window-screened. Sleeping porches for the
summer months, she guessed. The screens were always
bowed out and rusty and many were studded with cotton
balls to ward off flies.

    She had given her boys a bag of carrots. Her older
brother, now a minister in Little Rock, had a peculiar
way of eating a carrot when he was young. He would bite
carefully around the core. Did everyone but her know that
a carrot had a core? These days it seemed likely, given all
she'd missed, all that had gone on, all she was now being
blamed for. The core of the carrot is stark, spindly. It has
these little limbs; it resembles a tree scorched by a forest
fire. Her brother taught her how to core a carrot and

she passed the skill on to her children. In the back seat at that moment her two youngest boys were loudly and competitively at work. The final product they would lean forward to thrust in her face. She was to judge the most perfectly cored.

Her daughter was with her, also, but she hated carrots. Her two other children were old enough to stay home. She had left them there after dinner. Her husband did not come home from work. It was Tuesday and the paper he owned and ran almost single-handedly came out on Wednesday so she rarely saw him on Tuesdays, but since the trouble started she saw him hardly at all. He was the one who broke the story about the community college where she was dean of students. There were discrepancies in the numbers of students enrolled and those who actually took classes. Dummy enrollments. Someone was skimming the money. She knew it was the president of the college, whose doctorate was in Physical Education and who would soon quit to start a Toyota dealership with the money he stole, but she could not find proof of it, and nightly she fought with her husband who she thought should never have written the story in the first place, since of course suspicion fell on her, she was dean of students, no matter that enrollment was the province of the registrar. Yet she was in charge of recruitment, and since her husband had gone all Woodward and Bernstein, why would her coworkers *not* think she was his Deep Throat? Because of her they might lose their jobs.

And yet her husband was adamant about what he

called his ethical responsibility to write the truth. He knew she did not have anything to do with it but if he chose not to write about it (even though clearly there was a conflict of interest) it would seem all the more as if she were guilty. He took it all so seriously, his duty to afflict the comfortable, while she drove, more and more, nights and Saturdays, deep into the county to attempt to comfort the afflicted. She knew all the guidance counselors in the county and had them keep lists of kids who were smart but had no encouragement at home to do anything other than go to work in the fields or the blender factory or the chicken processing plants. Some of them had kids themselves. They thought their lives were over and it was her job to offer them a way out of these woods. She loved this part of her job the most. The more people assumed she'd made up students, the harder she scoured the countryside for kids who needed a chance, needed her to save them.

Sometimes she spoke to her brother down in Little Rock. I worry about the children, she said. You worry about everyone's children, he said in a way that made her think her recruiting was more important to her than the well-being of her own kids. It was true in a way. Her own children had options. She had options. She could quit and get her old job back at the high school, teaching Latin to the overachievers and Civics to those who would end up at the slaughterhouse, the blender factory. She didn't do anything wrong. Except this: all these people off down in the country kept dogs. She was terrified of dogs.

Dogs, of course, knew of her terror. She couldn't very well leave the three youngest alone nights when she went out recruiting was what she told herself, but in fact the oldest could have kept them from burning the house down. She placated them with carrots and coring contests but really she needed them to get out of the car and knock on the door if there were dogs.

That night they came to a place at the edge of the Black River. They were in an area called Six Run. Hardly anyone from this part of the county went on to the community college. Most of them, rumor had it, were intermarried. Never mind all that: they deserved a chance. But she needed bodies, real students, she needed to prove to everyone that the numbers might have been tampered with before but no longer. Her husband could fend for himself. Have another carrot, she said, passing the bag back to the boys. See who can make the prettiest tree. They pulled up to a house covered in lattice. The lattice was covered in vine. On the way in they had passed five or six cars abandoned in the woods. Someone had cut down trees to make little driveways for these abandoned cars but the trees had come back, growing through the engine blocks of hoodless Fords. This place is scary, said her daughter, looking up from her book.

She heard the dogs before she saw the house. The guidance counselor had told her about the girl who lived here. Bettina. She's shy as all get out but she's smart. Her parents won't let her speak to you, though. You might as well not bother. But she bothered. The barking dogs greeted them as they pulled into the clearing around the house. What if they broke the chains? The way they snarled, their hatred, their hunger. Get out and go knock on the door, she told her boys. They liked dogs, but these dogs? The boys pushed their faces against the window, staring. Go on, she said, give them a carrot. I'll give them mine, said the youngest. And they got out, clutching their carrots. Two of the dogs were somehow placated by her boys, but there was a third. Her daughter had put down her book and climbed in her lap to look. The boys held hands as the dog yanked at the end of his chain. That dog, she would tell her husband later. He knew what was going to happen when he lunged for my babies. He knew it was going to hurt. She didn't tell him how the youngest boy had held up his carrot and how she thought she'd seen, in the last light filtering through the leaves, the tiny limbs on the scorched tree. She told him only about the dog, knowing its fate, throwing himself over and again at her brave little babies, the chain tightening the collar, nearly strangling him each time.

Need Not

Rosemarie came out from the black bedroom at the end of the hall and said, Well, he's gone. The neighbor lady was over and she and my mother were visiting. They were catching up. I was lying on the floor pushing my milk truck over a mountain made of humped-up rug. My mother nodded at Rosemarie and the neighbor lady said, Well. Everyone was saying it so I said it. I said it to the man inside the truck. The milk man. Well, you're gone, I said to the milk man but no one was listening to me. I was four or maybe I was five. I could look it up, there must be some record of when he died, but what would be the point? I never knew him. My older sisters Rosemarie and Rita would not say anything about him whenever I asked. Well, what did he *do*? I asked Rita once when Carly and I were still off at that place they sent us to and Rita had quit school and gone to work at the telephone company to save enough to get us out of there. Fred who they said was my brother had driven her up to Raleigh to see us in the home. Mama it made her too sad she only came once. Fred said, He run two or was it three of mama's family farms into the ground. Fred, said Rita. Also he had him a shirt-pressing business. Gone make it big pressing somebody's shirt. He ran a store, said Rita. Right into the ground, said Fred.

My mother and the neighbor lady kept right on catching up. Rosemarie was standing there. She wasn't looking at anything. The neighbor lady talked about another neighbor lady and then she said about the new preacher at her church that he needed a shut off valve. I liked to burnt the pot roast cause of his going on and on. The neighbor lady never would change out of her housecoat. Well, he's gone, I said. I looked up at my mother. Rosemarie was sitting on the arm of my mother's chair and she was wiping her dripping nose. My mother reached over and took Rosemarie's arm and patted it. Rosemarie come to and started looking at things again. She looked at me. The neighbor lady said to Rosemarie, You did him good, child. Rosemarie did not look at the neighbor lady. I said something to the milkman who had got his truck stuck in a ditch and Rosemarie said for me to hush. She got up and went back down to the hallway to where he'd been lying there coughing. I would hear him in the night. Sometimes he would wake Carly whose crib was in my room and I would have to go wake mama who was sleeping in Fred's old room. Fred I have no idea where he slept. Me and Carly were in that place nearly a year when Rita came to pick us up and carry us home. How long was he in that room coughing I asked her? Fred was driving the delivery truck for Dusselbach's Furniture, the four of us squeezed on the one seat, Carly on my lap asking for ice cream. She didn't want to leave, she didn't

remember not living in that place, they bribed her out of
there saying she'd get a scoop. If memory serves, took the
bastard nearly a month to cough his lungs up, said Fred
and Rita got all over *me*. Quit asking your questions, she
said. We got you out of that awful place and we're all
going to be together again, mama's going to be so happy.
Why didn't she come get us then I wanted to ask but
Carly was crying wanting only the ice cream.

Whenever Rosemarie disappeared into that black
bedroom my mother said to the neighbor lady, He's put
me in right much of a mess. The neighbor lady said the
Good Lord will provide. My mother yawned. I can't feed
all these mouths, she said. The two babies. She stopped
talking and I felt her looking at me. She was seeing was
I alive. Because after Rosemarie said for me to be quiet I
played possum. I was asleep and so was Carly in her crib,
slept through the whole thing. I know, child, said the
neighbor lady, even though my mother was older than
her. You have to do what's right for all involved. Then
she changed the subject to a thunderstorm. My mother
didn't care about the thunderstorm (see, I did), she said
her icebox was broke. The neighbor lady said she could
see could her brother-in-law stop by to take a look at it
if they could catch him sober. My mother smiled but the
neighbor lady laughed. I was up under the house with
Rufus the dog. He didn't like thunder either. He would
go up under the house and dig a hole in the dirt and
scrunch down. He would be shivering. I was up under
there with him when my mother said, I best go tend to

him. I'll look after the young'un, said the neighbor lady. He's asleep, said my mother and I smiled. The neighbor lady must have seen me because as soon as my mother hauled herself out of her chair and made her slow way down the dark hallway, the neighbor lady leaned over and said, Boy, I need to tell you something. I made like I was dead. Now, your daddy, he has just passed, she said. I knew more of the man when he was alive than after he died when no one would answer my questions and the only thing I remember is him putting me on a horse one time at my aunt Virginia's farm and leading me around the pasture. He was smoking a cigar and I remember he said the smoke would shoo the flies. I coughed from the smoke and the horse coughed too. The neighbor lady was still leaning over me. Boy, she said. Did you hear what I said? Well, I said, Ought I to cry? I scooted up close to the neighbor lady, right under her nose. Well, I said, but it wasn't a question. Oh, honey, she said. You poor thing. You needn't cry. Do you know how to pray? God is great God is Good let us thank him for our food. That's a blessing, said the neighbor lady. That's not a prayer, it's a blessing. She looked at me like I ought to apologize but I didn't apologize and I did not cry and I did not think she deserved to know how hungry I was.

Never Mind

BECAUSE HE DID SOMETHING FOOLISH, a thoughtless act of vandalism, a boy was sent away to live with his aunt. He was from the coast and his aunt lived high in the Appalachians and at night outside his window he felt the looming of these black mounds against a truncated sky. The streets in his aunt's village were so curvy and steep that he had to walk down the hill, fair weather or foul, to meet the school bus. That he could not understand much of what the mountain kids said made him feel more the stranger. They left him alone for so long that he felt he had lived an entire lifetime without benefit of the milestones that he, even at fourteen, suspected were not always fulfilling: marriage, job, house, children, grandchildren, retirement. Still, he felt he deserved the opportunity to at least fuck these things up.

His aunt, who had taken him in because her husband had died young and she had no children of her own and the boy's parents thought she could use the company, seemed perplexed by his presence in her kitchen in night, where she sat at a table reading mysteries and drinking sherry and eating almonds. Sometimes she would remember to ask him about his day. One day in the early spring he got on the bus and there was an odor so noxious he had to breathe through his mouth for the forty-five minute ride through the hollows. With each new passenger the smell grew worse. It was present, too, in the classrooms, and in the cafeteria, so he took his lunch outside and ate watching the children in the adjacent elementary school throw their coats off and chase each other around the monkey bars. Maybe the odor was his own. The stench of loneliness, of making one bad choice and having to suffer for it. Perhaps a stint in juvenile hall would have been preferable to this isolation. The mountains were more formidable than chain link and razor wire, guard dogs or moats. The smell was absent in the blustery parking lot but returned once he entered the classroom. On the bus ride home he sat in the back and lowered the window, even though it was cold out, the clouds clinging to the hollows sending down a few final flurries of snow. That night he sat down to dinner with his aunt tentatively, scared she would not be able to eat because of the stink coming off of him, but she tucked into her stroganoff. Finally he said, Today there was this smell? What smell, she said, looking up from her plate. It was all over, he said, on the bus, in the hallway at school, in the classrooms. Well what did it smell like, his aunt asked him. The boy looked at his plate, then out the window. The sun had burned off the clouds but was setting now pinkly over the ridge, each tree visible like the hair on the overgrown ears of his grandfather just before he died. It was like, I don't know, sort of . . . The boy felt that everything depended upon his making his aunt understand something he was not even sure he had not made up. Like onions, he said, because he hated onions and his aunt kept forgetting that and put them raw in the salads she served him and did not notice when he picked around them. His aunt studied him for a minute, then returned to her meal. The boy felt he was being mean to his aunt and said, Never mind.

Years later she would write to him from the nursing home in a town just down the mountain from her village. He was married and he had two children and an okay job and he loved his wife but there were, as he had suspected at fourteen while sitting invisible on a school bus, no guarantees in the path he'd taken. He kept in touch with his aunt sporadically and always felt he should go visit her more because even though she'd had no idea what to do with him, this sullen quiet force who had taken up residence in her basement, she had been kind to him. He had lived with her for a year until his parents felt he had straightened himself out enough to return home. His aunt sent a postcard with a photo of the fountain in front of the courthouse in her village. He turned the postcard over to find, written in a careful if jerky hand:

RAMPS ! ! ! ! ! ! (LOCAL DELICACY)

He put the postcard in a drawer, convinced his aunt had lost or was losing her mind, and he promised himself he would go see her, but a few weeks later she died. He went alone to the funeral, as both his parents were dead and none of his siblings had been close to his aunt. He arrived early to the village, which appeared, of course, smaller, and drove around for awhile, remembering the loneliness he'd felt there, which seemed profound but also redemptive, as if the year he spent here—attending a mediocre school with kids who ignored him, living with this woman who fed him and bought him things his mother would never have allowed him to have—for instance, Dr. Pepper—and took him all the way to Asheville to see *Dr. Strangelove* and *M.A.S.H.*, had taught him something vital about what he might (or might not) expect out of life. But how could this be? He barely knew his aunt. After the funeral, he introduced himself to her neighbor, one of the two or three people he recognized, and, having soon run out of things to say about his aunt, mentioned the postcard he'd received from her just a few weeks earlier. Well I never eat 'em myself, said her neighbor, who unlike his aunt was a native of the region and spoke like it, but back in the day my daddy and his brothers would beat the woods clean of 'em come spring. It'd be ramps and taters and ramps with eggs and no thank you, I could never tolerate the smell.

He said goodbye to the neighbor and drove to the fountain in front of the courthouse featured in the postcard his aunt had sent him. He got out and sat on the low wall surrounding the fountain. He wondered if she'd been thinking about him and the answer had come to her, or if she had not thought of him in years and the answer had come to her, involuntarily, mysteriously, as if some window had opened in her memory and she was suddenly sitting at that table with him, her strange nephew who thought the smell was coming *from him.* It was dark—the last light filtered through the top of the mountain ridges—when he decided that his aunt had known he was scared, though she'd not found the words to tell him that he was right to be scared—she was scared herself—it was only that he was scared of all the wrong things.

Work Camp

THE THREE OF US walked to the end of the dirt road,
crossed the ditch and stood by the high chain link fence
of the prison yard. Slowly a few inmates drifted over.
They ain't in any hurry, said Pint. Nowhere to be, said
Darryl. It was Darryl's idea to go talk to them. Kicked
out of Boykin's store for ripping the felt of the pool
table with the cue, too broke to walk the mile into town
to buy a fifty-cent can of Bull from Big Betty Carter's
bootlegging stepdad. No swimming since a boy had been
bit by a moccasin in the irrigation pond old man Avery
dug to water his crops. Pint had gone and gotten his bike
stolen. Nothing to do and it was mid-nineties out and
the strings of our cut-off jeans clumped to our knees like
wet hair. I have an idea, said Darryl. He lived at the top
of the dirt lane that dead-ended at the ditch bordering
the prison yard. All three of us lived within a quarter
mile of it but I rarely noticed the men smoking on picnic
tables in the yard facing the highway. Sometimes when I
drove past with one of my sisters I would hear them wolf-
whistling or calling out Look Here Girl Hey Darling
but only at night, when I passed by and saw through the
barred windows the rows and rows of bunk beds, all those

men asleep or not asleep under the fluorescent lights, did I wonder about their lives, and then only because I slept in the tiny room with my two older brothers and there were fights nightly about turning the light off, my oldest brother (who had his own single bed across from our bunk bed) given to reading the World Book well past midnight.

Only in this way did I compare my life to theirs. My father had told us it was medium security, and he referred to it as the *work camp*. He said most of the men had stolen cars or robbed gas stations or gotten caught driving without a license but Pint swore there were murderers and rapists doing time there. That day three inmates came to the fence: two whites and a black. The whites wore their hair slicked back. It was 1973; the three of us wore our hair to our shoulders. Why is Marvin Gaye hanging with Sha Na Na? said Darryl. Look at the little ladies in they short shorts, said the black prisoner. Come closer so I can stick my dick between this fence for y'all to suck. Darryl laughed and said, Y'all see that metal shed up the road there? The prisoners looked over our heads as if Darryl had pointed out something beyond their comprehension. As if their world had shrunk to the confines of the yard and even the three of us, standing just yards away, were distant and vague. We can stash some street clothes behind it, said Darryl. The metal shed, sunstruck, shimmered. They squinted and drooled. Think I can fit in your panty-waist dungarees, said the white one who I realized was not much older than we were.

What you want for it, youngblood, said the black one.
Y'all got to be running some game. We ain't got no game
going, said Darryl, we just trying to help y'all out. Simple
business transaction's all we're talking about. And how do
you expect us to get to that shed, said the older white guy,
whose right bicep bore the word *Cindy* in spindly black
letters. What would you pay for me to chuck some bolt
cutters over this fence? Darryl said. Fuck these brats, said
the younger white guy, I ain't got but two months left on
this bullshit sentence and these little bitches going to set
y'all up. He took off in a lopsided strut. Motherfucker
cut somebody's throat in the parking lot of a pool hall
but of course he's all innocent, said Cindy's boyfriend.
So was I all innocent. Darryl's father would beat him
if he did not finish his chores and Pint's dad crashed
his car into the bridge over the Six Run River and six
months later his mother married Billy, the milkman,
and Billy did not even try to be somebody's daddy. My
parents just shrugged when I quit cropping tobacco for
Reboyd Warwick because it was too hard. All my father
said was, the migrants that took your place don't have
the option of walking off the job because it got too hot
up top the barn or someone spotted a copperhead. How
much you want? The black prisoner asked again. Twenty
for the bolt cutter, ten apiece for a change of clothes.
Shit, let's go to the bank and get these girls their money,
said the older one, but the black one looked at us like
we'd come suddenly into focus: Hey, y'all boys holding?
If we had any weed, would we be standing here talking

to y'all unlucky locked-up bitches? Darryl said. You best watch your mouth boy, said the older prisoner, I know exactly where you live. Then the guard spotted us from the tower. Move away from the fence, he said through the loudspeaker. I know where all y'all live, the man said as he backed away, looking at me.

That night I lay awake sweating, inches from the overhead light. Too scared to tell my brother to turn it off. First night in my life I remember not going to sleep at all. Even in the darkness I lay there listening. Years later Darryl would call me up to tell me Pint was dead. Hep C from a needle Darryl was trying to tell me the three of us had shared. You got me mixed up with someone else, I said. I was at the park watching my daughter cruise around the empty tennis court on her Big Wheel. This was not long before Darryl killed himself to keep from going back to prison. I didn't even know he went the first time. I watched my daughter, egged on by an older boy who lived down the street, pedal hard, straight for the net. I got to go, Darryl, I said, and hung up. Daddy, daddy, my daughter called, and I went to her even though I felt like maybe she might have gotten me mixed up with someone else.

Ghetto Teacher Film Festival

ON A TRAIN that morning she passed an abandoned basketball court on the crust of the city, and remembered the weekends she spent with her father after her parents divorced. His tiny apartment in a neighborhood near the college, ratty couches on front porches, late-night whooping and thumping music from student parties, the crusty men filling their grocery carts with cans that littered lawns the morning after. His apartment had only one bedroom, so she slept on a futon in the living room. The house was old and had a high narrow closet on one wall which, when opened, revealed a short ironing board, its ancient soiled cloth smelling of the inside of the canvas tent her father had once set up for her in the backyard of the house where her mother lived. At her mother's she had her own room, and places to put things: her clothes, her toys. Her father showed her another tiny closet built into the same wall by the ironing board, but it was too high for her to reach and not large enough for much more than a stuffed animal and her slinky. Also? It had no door.

What even went there, she asked, and her father said, I believe a phone. He said it in a way that made her think he wanted, now that he was living in this place, to have the right answer to every question she asked. But why put a phone in a closet?

Her father referred to the tiny closet as her cubby, because, he said, he was assigned a cubbyhole at school when he was her age and that is where he stored his things. What things? His rain slicker, he said, and his rulers, and those things you attached a tiny pencil to in order to draw a circle. The girl had no idea what he was talking about, but then it seemed to her that her father had, since moving out, begun to talk a lot about strange things that had happened to him when he was her age, or things he had once owned. In the morning she would lie on the futon and listen to him making coffee. He let her sleep far longer than he used to, and she thought, now, on the train, in a decrepit part of the city so far from where she grew up, in another part of the country in fact, that he did so because he had no idea what to do with her and was just as eager as she was for the weekend to pass, so that she could go back to her mother's where he knew she was far more comfortable and he could do whatever it was he did when she wasn't there.

During the long days he took her to the zoo, the historical museum, the park, the science center, the movies, ice-skating, roller-skating, to a boring baseball game where grown men rose in the bleachers to spell out letters to a song called YMCA. At night they walked to a video store staffed by girls with tattoos and checked out movies, always old ones he liked when he was a kid. They watched *To Kill A Mockingbird* twice in one weekend and she did not have the courage to tell him she hated black-and-white movies, that the grey world gave her nightmares in which the sun disappeared from the sky. At the end of *To Sir With Love* he told her about listening to the theme song of the movie on a transistor radio under his covers at night. The words he sang to this old song he liked so much he listened to it surreptitiously in the night smelled of beer.

We'll watch only movies like this, he said. Black and white? she said. No, he said, movies that prove you can actually make a difference in someone's life. It took her a couple of weekends to understand that what he meant was movies in which students were mean to new teachers. *Blackboard Jungle* was next, but at least the rest—*Stand and Deliver*, *Freedom Writers*, *Lean on Me*—were in color. There was always one kid everyone picked on and often there was a boy who carried a knife. These movies terrified her, but she understood that something in them made her father both sadder and stronger. She had never seen her father cry, but during *Music of the Heart*, her father nodded at her cubby and said, We are so lucky, sweet girl, we don't need nearly as much as we've been given. His nose ran and he wiped it on his sleeve.

On the bus in a part of the city as grey as the black-and-white movies her father favored, the girl, now a woman in her early thirties, thought of her father as a child in the back of a classroom steamed by radiators. Students threw desks and wrote filthy words on the blackboard and the teacher went home to his pregnant wife and broke down at the dinner table, but her father sat happily drawing circles with this device he had described to her that he did not seem to mind not knowing the name of, some obsolete instrument fixed with a pencil stub and a spike to anchor it always to the page.

I'm Coming Back to Love You Again

WHAT THE MEAGER RIVER where his ancestors had set up their fledging concern divided was nothingness and more nothingness. Scrub and swamp, cypress knees and dripping moss. You nearly had to get lost to even find the ferry crossing. Locals used it to visit cousins; the only nonnative passengers were families in minivans seeking an authentic experience that lasted only seven minutes and took them ninety miles out of their way. Across and back, east to west to east, morning to sundown. His bow was his stern, his stern his bow. Don't you ever grow weary, he was sometimes asked of his to-ing and fro-ing. But there was someone, once, across the river. When he first saw her they were in grade school and he was riding in the bed of his uncle's pickup. They passed her farmhouse and he saw her reading a book while lying on her back in the grass, her feet propped up on a swing hanging from the branch of a live oak. Years later he would meet her in town, on a side street. She would be waiting in the same place alongside the wall of a shoe store. Why do you always wait there, he asked her once just before he leaned in to kiss her and she said, because the sun warms these bricks and they keep the heat all day long and on into the night. That he never loved anyone more than her at that moment, that she came from the one side of the river and ended up living with him on the banks of the other was, he might have said if he had been inclined to say, enough, even though she'd long ago left him and taken his daughter and moved to Arkansas with a lineman who'd come north in a convoy of trucks to restore power to the region after a storm. Always, in every car bumping up the broken pavement leading to the landings, he looked for her, and so he kept on ferrying people across the river for the same price his father had charged, seven dollars, even though he could barely afford fuel. But he would never go up on his price, because it seemed to him that any more than a dollar a minute to go absolutely nowhere was kind of high.

Deep Eddy

WE HAD TO PARK by the bridge where the black ladies
fished through dusk on upturned plastic buckets, ignoring
us as they peered into the murk for the bob of red cork
in the water. A quarter-mile walk along a root-ruptured
path to where the water whirlpooled and the bottom
dropped so wildly, myth bubbled up from it, a froth of
dead babies crying on moon-shiny nights, suicide pacts
of numerous young lovers, an entire stagecoach of painted
ladies, midway from Charleston to Baltimore in pursuit
of a regiment of whoremongers, sucked under its current.
Sorcery, devilment, human sacrifice: legends spread for
decades by teenagers who heard them from grandmothers
trying any old lie to warn them away from a place known
for deflowering. But we went that night and other nights
seeking only the wild circling current. We'd just been to
see a movie where a dingo ate a baby, stole it from a tent
in the night while the parents slept alongside it, and we
were talking all Australian. Bye-bee, she called me, my
bye-bee. We went in with our underwear on, laughing at
our awful accents. She'd lost her flower with the first of
a string of boys and she liked me only in the way girls
like those boys who make them forget, temporarily, some

pain I hoped was only temporary. My job was to make her laugh. So we laughed at babies carted off by dogs on big grainy screens; we mocked the fantastic rumors of that cow-licked spot in the river and dubbed it Jacuzzi, we laughed at the word Jacuzzi, hollered it into the dark woods so we could laugh again at the echo. But the word rang in my head until it was frightening, not funny, so I told her something true that I knew she might misinterpret as the first line of a joke. Today I saw part of a snake. If she said, What part? I would swim to shore, pull on my clothes and leave. If she just said, Which? I would stop fighting the current and allow it to deliver me to her. Everything—then and since—hinged on a single word. There was no answer, just a gurgling in the dark water, laughter from the eternal circle of poor drowned whores, the baby in the dingo den, the short end of the snake.

I Got a Line on You

NOT ONE OF THE INHABITANTS of the town heard the train the girl named Claire touched in the night. They had grown used to the fury of its passage, had long since ceased to shift in sleep as it rattled window glass and, even at four in the morning, when only tumbleweed and tarantula risked the crossings, warned them with its whistle to stay clear. During the day the trains passed frequently, some of them double-stacked with shipping containers, their wild urban graffiti vibrant and shocking against the tawny hue of desert. The train Claire touched was longer than the town itself.

Claire had been drinking at Trudy's with a group of kids who worked the summer resorts—dude ranches and health spas—in the mountains northwest of town. They had been dancing to the golden oldies of a local outfit that called themselves Captain Hook and his Left Hand Band. They'd stayed on the dance floor until Captain Hook (Kyle Klunich, branch manager by day at Far West Pipefitters) closed out their set with an energetic, if ragged, version of Spirit's "I Got a Line on You." Trudy flicked the lights as soon as the applause died down. When the crowd spilled into the parking lot, Claire strolled over to a picnic bench beside the train track and sat. A coworker named Luke followed her over. He was curly haired and rough skinned, in love with Claire in a moony way that made her pity him and love him back, but not in the way he wanted. Far down the valley came the bleat of train. I am going to touch that train, said Claire. Me too, then, said Luke. The train entered town from the east. As the engine drew alongside the bench, Claire got up and walked toward it. Luke did not think she would keep walking. Later, he would claim he called out to her just before—not with a finger but with her entire hand, palm flattened as if to protect rather than to risk—Claire touched the train.

When the train—indifferent to the touch of anyone, even comely Claire—spun her toward and then away from its tracks, into the bed of recently laid gravel, Claire became a schoolgirl walking through an airport during the holiday crush, hugging a pillow to her chest. This was the way she used to imagine herself in an airport before, in her sophomore year in college, she flew to New York to visit a boy. On that first flight and every other one, the plane had smelled of its bathrooms and everyone who spoke over the intercom had done so with the same intonation. Flying, which should have been so wondrous—lifted above the earth and settled in some force that swept you in only minutes from the still-frozen prairieland of Minnesota to the early spring of Central Park—was so disappointing it was almost funny. Maybe this is what Claire was thinking as she was once again lifted above the earth. And maybe when she landed, it was not gravel she felt, but a fed-by-snowmelt lake across which she once swam naked with a boy so skittish in his disrobing and so awkward in his breaststroke that he would be, forever in her mind, chaste. Though she slept with him. He was her first. He loved her in the sloppy unrestrained way that Luke did, and like Luke, she could not love him back, but for a different reason: because she was just a teenager. Imagining Claire swimming in a fluid crawl across the frigid lake, pursued by the gangly ungraceful boy who loved her, don't you remember how things were back then? Don't you remember how we did things just to get them out of the way? Don't you remember how we left each other behind like outgrown band posters still hanging on the walls of the bedrooms we had inhabited since birth?

Rookies

BUT WHY DO WE HAVE TO DRESS UP like cops, I asked
Run. Because we'll make more money, he said. I met Run
at Mattie's. He was from Perquimans also but I never
knew him, nor his people. Years later after he died, I was
back home for a funeral and met one of his sisters who
told me they were raised Holiness and weren't allowed to
go into town except once a week to the tobacco market
on the back of their uncle's truck, each of the six set on
top of a burlap sack of tobacco to keep from losing a leaf
to the wind. At Mattie's one night both Dawn who was
Run's and June who was my girl were upstairs working
when Run said he knew how to make some quick money.
I ain't selling no more oregano to high school kids, but
okay, I said, and he told me about the bar in Newport
News and said about the uniforms, which weren't real
cop but security guard. Them Nellies love a man in a
uniform and will pay double, he said, so we would drive
over there and go stand at the bar for a few drinks so
they'd know we were off duty and then they'd come up
and start talking and we'd end up outside in the alley,
leaning against the bricks shoulder to shoulder smoking
and talking trash while they went to town on us. Run
could have gotten more than me had he been by himself

because I looked a couple times in the moonlight and saw he was thicker but we went together since most of these boys were sailors just into port and hardly any of them were what I'd of called a Nelly. Big strapping boys, some of them. Run said he'd heard of some would wipe off their lips with the back of their hand and reach in their pocket stick a knife to your throat to get their five dollars back. Don't ever get in a car with them, said Run, they'll drive you off somewhere and throw you in a basement and try to make you their husband or worse their wife. Ain't nobody going to make me their wife I said and Run said June will have you wearing an apron should you mess up and marry her. We never did tell Dawn or June how we were all of a sudden flush but neither of them when they found out after what happened with the vinyl-siding salesman seemed to have a problem with it. Neither ever complained about whoring, especially June who would tell me she loved me all day long but that she wasn't about to quit her job just because of a *feeling*. She said she loved fucking and she loved money so why not combine the two? Before that she had worked at the shipyard. I had too and so had Run but we all met at Mattie's. Dawn had *been* working there. One night Run and I were out in the alley with these two old peckerwoods. One of them said he sold siding. The one working on me never said a word. He was the shaky type like most of them until they heard that zipper coming on down the track and then there wasn't anything nervous about them. We'd been out there for a few minutes when all of a sudden Run called shot-cock violation. Say what, asked the vinyl-siding guy and Run who had drunk three ryes with Pabst backs, which meant it would of took him forever said, They's rules just like in basketball if I don't come in three minutes, you lose your turn. But I already paid you and goddamn if I don't want and Run pointed to his fake badge we bought at the dime store and asked did he want us to radio for backup, which got me to laughing, and the one working on me grabbed me by my hips to keep me still but he slammed my ass against the bricks when he done it so I pulled out and kneed him in the face hard. He took off down the alley. The vinyl-siding salesman started running his mouth about how we weren't real cops and everybody knew it and we weren't no different than them. Run said listen I am going to prove I'm different than you: I am going to slit your throat and leave you here to bleed out in this alleyway and no one would bother to come looking for me when they find out what you were out here doing. There is not a real cop would walk to the corner trying to find out who killed some traveling faggot. Soon as he said this I realized it was true. I guess I never thought about it before. I thought about June up under some old boy just got off second shift at the shipyard. She'd turned up at the house with bruises before but I never did try and talk her out of working for Mattie because I knew she would leave me. Still, what Run said to that man made me think I might go to hell if I didn't at least try, so I left Run in the alleyway arguing with the vinyl-siding salesman and I wasn't there when

Run beat him and took his wallet and his car keys. I was on a bus back to Mattie's when the cops pulled Run over in the salesman's Corvair and he tried to claim he worked security at the shipyard. Wearing a dime-store badge and goddamn dingo boots, his hair grazing his collar. Lying to a cop about being a half-ass cop as if a real cop gave a damn about a security guard, which was just some loser couldn't pass the PE test they give you at the rookie academy. The vinyl-siding salesman all he had to do was turn the whole thing around and put Run down on his knees in the alleyway. It didn't make him look any too good but since Run beat him all to hell and the man was from Ohio or Iowa or somewhere the judge declined to have him up on a morals charge. Dawn says for you to go talk to some lawyer about Run, June told me the next night but what was I going to say that wouldn't put me playing dress-up in a alleyway and maybe bring that old boy out of the woodwork whose nose I'd bloodied? And me end up in the cell with Run and get sent off like he did? A group tried to hold him down in the shower and make him into a wife. That's when he died. The night he said for us to dress up like cops I told him I had a sailor suit when I was little. Run said he wanted one but instead he had to settle for a towel he used as a cape to fly off the back porch. He said it was blue and white striped and he claimed to have saved it. You take it to the beach and lie out in the sun on it I asked. Run said he would never, he said he kept it rolled up tight, he said he kept it somewhere only he knew where.

Stragglers

THEN THIS GUY COMES UP to me as I'm standing in the parking lot finishing my cigarette.

They start already, he asks me. His voice was low and raw, like he'd been sick or something.

I did what Tory called my nod-shrug, my maybe-maybe-not-but-what-do-I-care gesture. She had other names for it. She said she couldn't understand me in the winter because I mainly talked with my shoulders.

You got another one of those, the guy says.

You can say no to yourself and others. But I pulled the pack out and shook one toward him.

You need a light too, don't you, I said, and he grinned, filter between his teeth, while I patted my pockets for matches. I wasn't really looking at the guy's face, but I was working at the Conoco station back then, and because it was boring selling gas and pop and cigarettes all day, I would watch people when they came in and note their height on the strip lining the door jamb. I had got to where I could guess within an inch. This guy was 6'1. Stringy.

Hey, you know that girl Tory?

I could hear chairs scraping inside. Chair scraping's like a guy clearing his throat before he makes his speech.

Last call, pretty much.

She's my sister, I said. Because sometimes I just say shit, to myself and others.

Oh, man, I'm sorry, he said.

Why are you sorry? All you did was ask me do I know her.

I wouldn't like some strange dude coming up to me bumming a smoke then asking about my sister.

Why not? I said. He looked at me and turned his head and blew smoke down the stairs toward the basement door, like he was *in* the basement already and he wasn't supposed to be smoking in there and he was blowing it out the window. I knew what he was going to say before he said it. The way he smoked, like he was getting away with something but worried he wasn't, made me anxious. He wasn't talking, so I felt like I had to.

So I said it for him: Because she's your sister, right?

Yeah, how'd you know?

How did I know what?

That Tory is my sister. Not *your* sister. Mine.

Tory never mentioned any brother. She just talked about her sister who was married to the guidance counselor at the high school. Beth. Of course she hated Beth because I wasn't a guidance counselor. Neither was this dude. I looked at him for the first time, or tried to. The sun was almost down and he wore a hoodie, which made his neck appear thicker than it was. His face was hard to see even though he was standing close enough to blow smoke on me. Maybe a little in the eyes? Hers were brown, though, and deep set. I studied his nose. Definitely not the same nose.

Tory never said she had a brother, I said.

Yeah? She certainly said some things about you.

I met Tory in the rooms, but we'd spent more time out of them than in. Now she wanted what she called a necklace. String together some days. She'd been talking about it. I knew I couldn't be standing in the parking lot and her inside and us still take the bus home. I also knew this guy wasn't her brother any more than I was. He was her new ride home.

I wouldn't say y'all favor, I said.

He took a drag of his cigarette—*my* cigarette, actually—and flicked it into the parking lot. That parking lot, any parking lot, a thousand parking lots. Freshly paved, potholed, enclosed by chain link fencing or shrubs, hemmed in by buildings too tall to see the tops of, opening onto a park or a forest or a lake. How is it that so much of my life has been spent in parking lots and I don't even own a car? Always waiting for something or someone. Meet me in the parking lot at four, after work, before supper, I'll be by there, we're on our way. Heat wavy pavement, an inch of exhaust-blackened ice.

Different fathers, he said. He might have thrown me off earlier, but he was in my parking lot. I'd seen the likes of him, in parking lots from Tallahassee to Spokane. But I'd never seen him around Richmond before. His different father must have scooted. That's what different fathers do: make way for a new different father.

So does that mean she's step, or half? I asked, and before he could answer I said, Also, man, what exactly is a first cousin once removed? Who removed your cousin? The cousin removers? I guess they only had to remove his ass once, am I right?

He had stopped smoking to look at me.

Cousin removers all up in his face, I said. Don't you make me come back down here, cuz.

Jesus, he said, she was right.

Yeah she was. She's always right. And she's right inside. Do you want to go in there and say hi?

He looked almost ashamed then. I thought I had him. But then he started blinking and looking beyond, just like Tory had done when we'd got in a fight earlier waiting for the bus and I told her fuck it I'll take the next one go ahead I'll meet you.

I don't like everybody looking at me, said Tory's brother.

You want me to go in with you? I said. He nodded, and we walked down the stairwell, which was covered with wet leaves so thick you couldn't see the drain at the bottom. I opened the door and stuck my hand out like, you first. You can say no to yourself and to others. As he squeezed past me he whispered, she was right about you. She was watching from her folding chair. She had her arms crossed. Blinking. She was looking beyond me, at the door, which took forever to close.

Sunday in the Blue Law Bible Belt

HE WANTED A DRINK, but he'd sat up late in the backyard with his neighbor and the recycling bin was filled with empties. Local ordinance gave the liquor-store clerks the day off. Why do people drive so slow on their way home from church, he asked his wife, who was lying on the couch watching a television series, one episode after another, wrapped in an afghan, drinking tea. She had gone to bed at some point; he wasn't sure what point that was, exactly. When she did not answer his question, he thought of the wine-flushed woman he'd met at a gallery opening, who had put a name to what he knew was coming: *hammers*, she called them, those shadowy regrets you suffer after a night of blistering drink, tapping away at your conscience while you wait anxiously to be held accountable for things you said or did that you do not remember. I guess I could go to church and find out, he said. His wife did not look up from the television, on which a male and female detective traded sexy insults while running their unmarked car through a car wash. The noise of the jets pounding the cop car hammered away at him also. He could look at it this way: it's not such a bad thing to lose a snippet of his life during which his behavior was less than exemplary. Or he could take the long view: in a year, neither of them would remember this night, and in ten years, the memory of this rental house would need to be summoned by a snapshot in a photo album. He was reminded of eloquent phrases great thinkers had conjured to explain the weight of the past. *History is a nightmare from which we are trying to awake. Those who fail to understand the past are doomed to repeat it.* Neither of these quite did it for him. He said to his wife, Do you think preachers maybe remind everyone to obey the speed limit as they're leaving the sanctuary?

She was going to make him wait; she liked to see him suffer. She wanted to keep him mired in the moment when he did whatever he did, even if he did not remember it. Especially if he did not remember it. But whatever he had done was history. History is that hammer, hurled through time and space, from that place we do not remember. See? His definition came close to rhyme. His wits were never dull on his mornings after; he might feel physically wretched but his mind would be vibrantly alive. How deeply he felt the world! He loved his wife so much he felt a slight pain on the enamel of his front two teeth. He didn't like to watch television during the day, though—he found it depressing, especially when hungover—so he went out on the porch. He sat on the stoop, watching the parade of probably Baptists, who had voted to keep the Sabbath free of alcohol, roll slowly by. They had passed their blue law for people like him, but it made him only thirstier. He would strain shaving cream, drink the juice of fermented fruit, if he did not know (in that place where we know the things we cannot bring ourselves to say) that history is not the hammer, as he had so glibly deduced a few minutes earlier, but that moment where you give in to the hair of the dog because you can no longer stand the hammering.

Typingpool

AT THE WEDDING RECEPTION the woman no one knew waited in the receiving line. She had arrived carrying a large green trash bag of the type intended for grass clippings and raked leaves. Since joining the line, she had rested the bag on the floor of the hotel ballroom, and propelled it along, as the line moved slowly toward the newlyweds, with her feet. She spoke to the lady behind her in line approvingly of the bride's gown and they chatted about the fact that among the ushers there was a woman, reportedly a close friend of the groom. How forward thinking, they agreed. Neither the woman behind the woman with the bag, nor the man in front, whose leg she accidentally brushed with her bag as the line lurched suddenly to a halt, asked if she was a friend of the bride or the groom. She was glad for that. She was prepared to answer, should it come up, the question of why she was there, but her answer would not be in words but in the unveiling of what lay at her feet, covered in green plastic. And then she was three or four people away from the couple and then next in line. No one else had brought presents through the receiving line—there was a table in the corner piled high with brightly wrapped boxes, but it was not meant for her, for her gift. She studied the smiles of the bride and groom but she did not listen to the exchanges between them and the people who were congratulating them in the most ordinary and obvious ways. Then she was standing in front of them. She turned to the woman with whom she had been discussing the female usher.

I wonder if you would help me with something?

The woman smiled at the bride and groom and their own smiles, held so long, began to dim. They studied her closely, as if trying to place her. She was bending over and pulling something out of her bag. A quilt. She handed two corners of the quilt to the woman who had agreed without actually agreeing to assist her, and she took two corners herself and stepped back so that the entire quilt was taut and visible. Those in line behind her watched curiously.

The woman said, My husband fought in the war. We'd been married for nine months when he got called up. It was April of 1944 and my husband had a year of college and knew how to type and every night in bed before he left I would pray and my prayer would be only two words, which in my anxiety I shortened into one: Typingpool, Typingpool.

The woman stopped talking and laughed. Her laugh was so clear and unexpected that it seemed she was genuinely amused.

Can you imagine a less effective prayer? Anyway, it didn't work.

She looked at the quilt, and everyone else did too,

except for the bride, who had grown visibly nervous and was sending her husband who-is-this-woman looks.

He was assigned to the infantry and sent to Germany, the woman said. His regiment entered the country near Aachen in September and a few days before Thanksgiving they dug in at the edge of a pasture and built fortifications and exchanged artillery and mortar rounds with the Germans.

The woman looked around at the guests and said, Goodness, I hope none of you are of German stock. Anyway, on November 24th, around noon, an artillery shell, fired by the Germans, exploded in the forest before hitting the ground. The trees in the forest literally exploded!

She pointed to the quilt. Here are the fortifications I spoke about, she said, nodding toward the edge of the quilt at a line of brown rectangles, and here, surrounding the pasture, which you will note is not green, because it was winter there, is the forest.

The groom studied the quilt. The trees in the forest were many and intricately detailed. The woman had stitched veins in their leaves resembling maps of tributary systems. The bride looked around the room frantically for her father, who she spotted in his tux, clutching his fourth or fifth drink, oblivious in the far corner, laughing with a red-faced friend.

The woman pointed to needle-like stitches hailing down upon the pasture from the forest. The shelled trees, as they disintegrated, sent slivers everywhere, she said.

My husband took a piece of wood in his heart. Can you imagine? A little splinter! Pierced in exactly the wrong place!

In the center of the quilt lay a soldier, his gun still shouldered, with a thin brown shard protruding from his chest, red thread surrounding the wound.

No medic could have saved him.

The woman took the ends of the quilt from her assistant and folded it in the way honor guards fold flags. She pressed it to her heart and said, I have long made my peace, and then she presented the quilt to the newlyweds.

Thank you, said the groom as he took the quilt from her.

Now who are you again? asked the bride.

The woman said to the groom, You're quite welcome. She spotted a man in a suit—not the sort of suit you'd wear to a wedding, but the sort you'd wear to work in an insurance agency—hurrying toward her. She smiled once again at the couple and walked to the man and offered him her elbow, as if he were her escort.

Who *was* that? said the bride. What in the hell was that? The groom did not answer because he was not listening. He was marveling over the amount of stitching the woman had put into that quilt. The nights and nights the woman had spent alone, laboring over the depiction of a forest and a field in a country she'd never seen.

Jack? said the bride. Here's Mr. and Mrs. Cooper!

The groom shook Mr. Cooper's hand, but beyond the bandstand he saw artillery light the pasture. He felt ground shaking as trees disintegrated. He hadn't even been alive when the Germans shelled the tree but it wasn't that long ago, really.

For years when his wife would tell the story of the awful thing that happened at their wedding, the groom would think of how that woman's life overlapped with his and how so much had happened to her, and he would want to interrupt his wife and make this point. But every time his wife told the story of the awful quilt incident—and it got told often, at cocktail parties and family gatherings and backyard cookouts—and she would call upon him to fill in details, he would say, You're doing great, honey, you don't need my help.

One night his wife was telling the story at dinner to some new neighbors. The wife of the new couple was an art historian.

I'm sure that must have been horribly uncomfortable but I have to say that the quilt sounds marvelous, said the art historian. And potentially quite valuable.

Valuable *how?* said the wife.

The art historian said, Vernacular artifacts of that sort—especially when we know the story behind them, and the quilter is not a professional—are collected by some of the best museums in the country. I'd love to take a look at it if I may.

Oh, I made Jack get rid of that thing right after we got back from the honeymoon, said his wife.

But he hadn't gotten rid of it. He had hidden it

among the rafters in the attic. He never looked at it and he would never, ever sell it, but every night he slept a little better knowing it was there, a story stitched together by the vigilance of memory and devotion, while the story of how they happened to come upon it, every time it got told, moved further and further from the truth.

Concession

IT WAS SAID about the blind woman who ran the concession stand in the lobby of the county courthouse that she could tell by touch the difference between a one and a five dollar bill. Judges, lawyers, felons, and their long-suffering kin spoke of her so-called sixth sense. She was aware of the rumor, which she attributed to ignorance. She understood why people might wonder not only how a blind woman managed to get on all by herself in this world but specifically how she managed to make a living selling nabs and peanuts and Sprites to a clientele most likely to cheat her out of an honest buck: judges, lawyers, felons, and their long-suffering kin. Money, to her, was dirty paper. She did not care for the feel of it and of course she could divine no difference between denominations. It was the breathing of her dog, Heath, stretched out on the tile beneath her feet, which prompted her to accept or reject a bill. Heath could smell a cheat. To Heath she owed most everything. He allowed her to live on her own, guiding her the three blocks between her apartment and the courthouse. He knew the way to the market, the beauty parlor. Without him, she'd be back living with her sister Edna and those four kids and her surly brother-in-law Kirk. Without Heath. All because of Heath. And yet he beyond irritated her, Heath. She sometimes maybe despised him just a little. Always on the job, always right. Knew the way, kept her safe, kept her lying, thieving, cheating, murdering clients honest. Go sleep in the kitchen, she said to him some nights as he panted on the rug by her bed. She had been known to say uglier things. In public, though—at work—she was all sugar, feeding him treats and using her aren't-you-a-sweetie voice, which she copied from Edna back when Edna had her first child and was still thinking babies were cute. Would they even believe her if she said it was Heath had the magic? They look at her and see a woman rescued, a woman who, Heath-less would be at the mercy of her family or the state.

But one day a boy—he sounded like he might be in his late teens—came up and asked could he pet Heath. She said what she always said, no matter who asked: unlike you or me, he can work and get rubbed on at the same time. She felt the boy bend to pet Heath and heard Heath's breathing alter before deciding the boy was okay, but the boy said something so purely surprising it rose right up to her: What do you reckon he dreams about? She listened to Heath's ragged breath. She thought about him panting by her bed at night. A blind woman dreamed same as a sighted one. Why not a dog? He never did get to run loose. She let him off his leash. He ran amok in what she'd heard books call the wilderness. In a pasture he chased some cows. He came to a creek. He leapt and he bounded, taunting squirrels and bees. It did not appear to bother Heath that he'd never catch the squirrel, the moth, the next-door cat. In his dreams, purpose had no place, nor did time or anything that reminded him of the leash tethering him to his charge. The boy's voice rose again like a blast of cold air from the courthouse door sighing slowly closed in winter. He wanted to know, now, what she thought Heath was dreaming about. It seemed to bother the boy, her silence. She felt that not even hazarding a guess about Heath's dreams was perhaps her highest form of respect. But she said, He's dreaming he's at a party and all of a sudden he is so tired he can't stand up and the hostess puts him in the back bedroom with all the coats and lets him sleep it off. When he wakes up, he tries to call her name—it's Laura—loud as he can, but no sound comes out. Finally she comes to check on him and he tells her his sister gave him an aspirin but it must have been some kind of dope. Laura doesn't believe him and he wishes he'd never said anything about dope. He gets her to help him up off the bed but he's all bent over still. His head's lying on his shoulder like it's broken.

She stopped. She thought the boy would say, Wait: he has a man's dream instead of a dog's dream? Because most people would assume she did not know about the back bedrooms at parties where all the coats were tossed, she readied herself with her answer, which was, Of Course, Why Not? But the boy, whose voice was no longer floating up to her but seemed to ricochet off the tile floor of the lobby, said, Oh, yeah. That's the one where when you finally wake up you realize it's *you* been trying to wake up for real. There isn't any party or Laura and you definitely don't got a sister. The blind woman reached out her hand for her dog. Her heart settled when she felt his hot breath on her palm. But the pill's real, said the boy. How's that, she asked him, and he said, first of all, no dream is all the way made up and second, people are always trying to slip you something when you're not paying attention.

Beamon's Woods

Every day but Sunday he dresses in the uniform of his former profession: Red Camel khaki-colored work clothes, steel-toed brogans, a thin windbreaker zipped to the Adam's apple if there is a shadowy sweetness in the morning breeze. He rises before dawn, lights the pilot of the kerosene stove in winter, lets the dogs out, careful not to slap the screen door. He sits at the kitchen table drinking instant coffee, black, from the same Styrofoam cup, for an hour until his wife rises and fries breakfast wordlessly in her housecoat. Neither of his sons wanted to take over the farm and his daughter moved up to Raleigh to work in a bank and he doesn't understand a good three-quarters of the things he hears people say. Commercials on television perplex him. There doesn't seem to be any logic to them; they begin in the middle and it's never quite clear to him what it is they're even advertising. He stands in the backyard looking out over the fields he leases now to an outfit out of by God Delaware, working a pick between his teeth, dogs at his feet. Maybe I have outlived time. Soon there will be no such thing as dew, the thing he once had to rouse himself early from bed to beat. Get it done before the sun burns the dew off. They'll do away with it, too. In the war he had been walking through a French forest pretending he was back home quail hunting in Beamon's woods with his cousins when he took two bullets: one through the palm of his hand, another in the shoulder, shattering his clavicle. The Germans pinned them down at the edge of a field for sixteen hours. Mortar rounds exploded the trees above him, turning tree limbs into tiny, deadly slivers. It grew dark and so cold he bit a wadded-up sleeve to quiet the chatter of his teeth. He lay there hoping he would freeze to death before he bled out because he had heard a frozen man just fell finally asleep. But some old boy came along, picked him up and slung him over his shoulder like a sack of fertilizer, took him deeper into the woods. He laid him down and stripped off his clothes and bound his wounds with tourniquets. Then he took his own clothes off and zipped two bags together and because of the heat coming off that boy's body, here he was, back home, pondering the disappearance of dew. He'd only been with his wife, one woman in seventy years, and all he had to compare the feel of her body to on a morning when the windows were frosty and the radiators clanked on was that boy, who was all muscle and hairy. It felt like a sin to still retain the memory of the roughness of the boy's cheek when in the night it grazed the back of his neck, but this wasn't the worst thing, nor was getting shot at and lying alone in the cold and dark trying to choose which way to die. Later, by the time he got back across the water to France, Hitler was dead. He figured the whole thing was over and he could go on home. Instead they sent him to supervise the POWs whose job it was to clean up one of those camps. Dachau. He saw a lot of things during that detail he'd just soon forget, worse things than when he was getting shot at, but it wasn't what they hauled out of there that got to him. After they'd liberated the place, men and women were camped outside the gates. His captain sent him around with an interpreter to tell them they were free to leave, but the next morning there they were again, sitting around a fire, dirty, skinny as saplings, eating the C-rations they gave them. Morning after that, same thing. He asked his captain why they were still there. Roma, he said. Gypsies. They ain't got no home. Here's as good as the next place to them.

Only the Horse Knew the Way

In the morning the girls' mother pinned the blanket around her two daughters and slapped the horse's croup. The older daughter held the reins and the younger daughter wrapped her arms around her sister's waist and both girls shut their eyes against the icy wind of the Nebraska plains. At the schoolhouse the teacher unpinned the blanket and later re-wrapped and pinned it again for the girls' journey home. The younger girl loved the outdoors and in the summer played barefoot in the fields with the boys from a neighboring farm, while the older sister spent hours in her parents' bedroom, brushing her hair with her mother's pearl-handled brush, counting her strokes as she pursed her lips in front of her mother's pearl-handled mirror. There was no money for college so the sisters took turns teaching school, one working a year while the other studied at the university. The younger sister, forever weary of chalk dust and spelling tests, saved enough to buy a piano and gave lessons in the parlor of her parents' home. Though she claimed she had no talent for teaching, she was patient with even the most tin-eared of her students because the scales they mangled at least contained notes, so much preferable to her than words. The older sister answered an ad calling for teachers to come to Wyoming. I shall only stay a year, she said to her younger sister at the train station, but she met and soon after married a rancher, who took her to live on his family's spread. Forty miles to the nearest town. In the summer she kept her children inside for fear they would be bit by rattlers, which were plentiful, until her husband convinced her to release the children to him, as they were needed to help with chores. It took an acre to raise one cow. There was so little rain she could grow only rhubarb, which could thrive, she discovered, on dishwater. Meanwhile, her sister met and married a slim, eager boy sent fresh from seminary to minister to the homesteaders. The younger sister played the piano in his church and he told her she played with a spirit unyielding. Within weeks of their wedding, they moved back east where the minister had family in the foothills of the Blue Ridge. Soon they filled the manse with their own brood. The two sisters spoke in their letters of childrearing. The older sister described the wind of the high plains and the younger sister spoke of the sinners her husband tended to, and in her description of sodden men who drank patent medicine manufactured for women suffering from monthly discomfort was a spark not present in her older sister's recounting of snowfall and drought. Thirty years of letters, birthday and Christmas cards. The younger sister's husband rode circuit to tiny churches deep into the mountains, leaving her to care for her children for days; the older sister's husband left the ranch only to travel to town, and spent every night of their marriage alongside her in bed. When her oldest son could drive, the younger sister convinced her husband to allow the assistant minister to take over for a month. They headed west in high summer, into heat that seemed to radiate from the miles first of flat field and pasture, then rock, sand, and bald mountains. They had planned to stay on the ranch for two weeks but there was no electricity and the water pumped from the well tasted of sulfur and the younger sister was so fearful of snakes on her hurried trips to the outhouse that she begged her husband to make up an excuse involving his duties so that they might leave after three days. But the preacher would not lie for his wife and instead announced that they were unaccustomed to this particular way of life and though it shamed them both to have acclimated to fineries unavailable to others, especially blood kin, nevertheless they would be departing at daybreak. The rancher wished them safe travels but the older sister said to the younger, Well, *you* were always the tomboy. Four years passed with no communication between the sisters. Then one day a telegram was delivered to the manse. Will arrive 5 o'clock p.m. Eastern Standard 21 May Hickory Station. The younger sister's husband blessed the reunion nightly for two weeks with special mealtime prayers. On the ride from the train station the older sister answered all questions tersely and excused herself for a nap as soon as they reached the manse. When she came down for supper she asked that the drapes be drawn, even though it was warm out and pulling the curtains to would hinder any breeze. The younger sister decided that her sister's sight was failing, that the brightness gave her headaches, but when she said as much, the older sister said, Brightness? It is much like a cave in this place. Where is the sky? All these trees, the way they sway in the wind. As if they are going to topple. And the houses so close together. The younger sister decided that her sister was trying to make her feel bad for rejecting the crude accommodations of her ranch; she wondered if this was why she had turned up—to claim that the lushness of foliage and shrubbery, the greenness of God's earth, was oppressive and somehow an indulgence. She couldn't very well criticize the indoor plumbing, the younger sister said to her husband, who attempted to argue that people are changed by places, that the elements can alter one's sensibility. This line of reasoning struck the younger sister as odd coming from a man of the cloth—aren't we all God's children? And this was her only living kin. For the rest of her visit, the sisters spoke sparingly and barely looked each other in the eye, though later, apart forever, each would sometimes remember being wrapped in the blanket all those years ago and set atop the horse. In the icy wind, the girls squeezed their eyes shut so tightly it gave them headaches, but neither minded that the words they sang into each other's ears to ease their journey were lost to the blowing snow.

The Frontier

ALONG THE QUIET STREETS they walked. Not until she was startled by an automatic sprinkler hissing awake did she grab his arm and then they talked about the click that precedes the switching on of heat or air conditioning in the houses where they grew up and how they found unnerving the half-second between that click and the whoosh of air through vents. He did not realize that this was exactly, and only, what he wanted to be talking about until, of course, they were talking about it. Then she told him that after her parents' divorce she had spent every other weekend with her father in a faded Victorian cut up badly into apartments in a dicey section of Philadelphia and every time the heat came on her father would announce, in the voice of a carnival barker, Ladies and Gentlemen, coming to us all the way from the basement, please welcome, with no further adieu, THE HEAT!

Everything he thought to say, or ask—did that joke ever get old, is your father still alive, what part of Philadelphia—seemed wrong, so he said nothing. Quickly his awkwardness was overcome by the righteousness of being so out in the open with her. The world slept but they walked right down the middle of it. The first hours of any new love should be conducted outdoors in the middle of the night, for powerful and lasting is the impression that you and your lover are moving together toward (and discovering alone) light.

Now you tell me a story, she said. He missed the hiss of sprinkler; he wished for siren. What to say next? Should he tell her that he had been living on a friend's couch, having lost everything in a fire started by his neighbor in 1-A, who had read in the paper that you should microwave your dirty sponges to kill germs and, when the sponge caught fire, only *thought* she soaked it thoroughly before tossing it in the trash and heading out to her shift at Olive Garden? Surely she would ask what he missed the most out of all he lost and he would have to say that records and even books were replaceable but that he would forever mourn the loss of the green t-shirt his favorite hippie uncle had given him, with an outline of the state of Virginia on it, beneath which was printed the question IS YOUR FUTURE AN ACCIDENT? Which had something to do with nuclear power, on everyone's mind at the time that his uncle bought the t-shirt, though all he would miss about it was the way it hung, loose but defiant, from his shoulders, as he put no real stock in the future, which might be something he'd have to explain to her, and in explaining to her his indifference toward the future, he might give her the impression that this—their meeting by chance in the kitchen of a party hosted by people that neither of them knew, thus allowing them to bond based on their both being outsiders, and escape to the outside—was hit-and-run. When, in fact, he wanted the night to last, for the two of them to find a park where there was a lake they could hear but not see lapping at shore and there they would kiss so that thereafter forever their kisses would be accompanied by a lullaby of water nearby but invisible.

Instead he told her about a book he was reading about German children kidnapped by Comanche on the frontier of what is now Texas and how the German children were taught by their captors to eat raw meat and think in another language and if they escaped or were rescued they were never free because they were ruined forever for Texas or America. When he finished there was only the hum of a streetlight they were passing under and he worried that she might be one of those people—he was one himself—allergic to plot summary. But instead she asked a question: What I want to know is, what would an Indian want with a German in the first place?

That it was a good question did not mean he knew how to answer it. He could say that the Indians had every right to kidnap and even kill Germans because after all it was their land and we Americans had freshly stolen it from Mexico, etc. But this answer seemed a dead-certain buzz kill. The world they walked through—right down the middle of—was theirs alone. Why bring ancient political injustices into it? He should have gone with the sponge, but here he was, trying to think of something funny to say. Don't *you* want a German? Why would they *not* want a German? But what if she was German on her mother's side? Or her father's? She had an Irish surname, but that didn't mean anything. He grew so self-conscious he could feel his eyebrows. Was he wearing a belt? Did people his age wear belts? He could answer her question by posing another. Are you wearing a belt? But women were not usually fans of belts. Their bodies were shaped such that a belt was usually not necessary. Unless, of course, it was an accessory.

He stopped walking. She took another couple of steps. When she stopped she was still close enough for him to lean over and grab her belt loop. He pulled her into him. The future, Germans, belts: What was wrong with him? He had always been this way, but she made him even more crazy dumb. However, he knew some things. They were so true he did not need to say them. There wasn't a body of water larger than a swimming pool within miles, so no soundtrack would ever accompany their first kiss. They did not escape anything when they found each other and walked out into the night, nor would they now be free. But they had rescued each other. And they were—already, before he even kissed her, he knew it was true—ruined for far more than Texas.

Hold On

AFTER SHE HAD HER LAST STROKE, the one that landed her pretty much day and night in her recliner, I bought her a television to put in her bedroom, first she'd ever owned with a remote. She held onto that clicker as if it were her first ever doll baby, carved from a corncob by her daddy before the dust kicked up and blew them out of the Panhandle. She turned that piece of Japanese plastic with all the buttons into something she was familiar with, something she'd lost but kept alive in her mind, a shining memory from darker days. All day long I hear her in there listening not to the words of the sermons but the auctioneer song of the preacher selling salvation. It could be a river pounding a rock. Rain on the tin roof of the house where she'd lived for sixty years of marriage. When I put that remote in her hand, she looked up at me and said, as if this were the only thing she had ever needed, What must I mash to listen to the pretty preaching?

Clearly the System Has Failed

SOMEHOW, FIRST SEMESTER of his junior year in high school, he ended up in a class called Business Machines. Some sort of scheduling error, as he was college prep, and normally placed in what were known as the accelerated classes, which referred not to the rate at which the learning progressed, but to the fact that in that long-ago era (this was 1975), students were deemed either bright or slow. The Business Machines classroom was located in the Vo-Ag wing of the school, which housed also Home Ec, Cosmetology, Carpentry, Auto Mechanics. The hallways smelled of oil burning off an engine block, of hair lathered with chemicals and fried beneath spaceman helmets. He had never been in this part of the school. He knew no one in the classroom. All but three of them were girls and the boys already had their heads on their desks. They looked him over first with derision for his dress—hair to his shoulders, new Levi's, a blue pocket tee, Wallabees—and then with dismissal, which led him to decide, more out of defensiveness than snobbery (for he was not, despite his destiny, a stuck-up kid), that in two years, half of the class would be making blenders on the assembly line out at Hamilton Beach.

He could have walked out. Gone to the guidance

office, informed them of the mistake. But something about all those machines lined up in the back of the room, carefully placed on high counters, machines he would learn the names and purposes of—the ten-key adding machine, two or three types of cash register, several brands of electric typewriters, a Dictaphone—made him take a seat instead. He raised his hand when the teacher, a woman with a high, dyed pile of hair and an efficient demeanor (Miss Southerland, he found her immediately exotic, for she called the roll as if she were leading the class in the pledge of allegiance), said his name. But within minutes they took a typing test and some mild attack of dyslexia (or nerves, as the rest of the class typed as if their machines were stalled on the tracks of an oncoming bullet train and only their flurrying fingers could save them from certain death) caused him to transpose a letter in his first name. Thereafter he was called, by Miss Southerland and by the surly girls who rarely referred to him at all, Cable instead of Caleb. Which he did not mind. Which in fact he loved. A new name seemed mandatory since Business Machines was its own zip code. Though it shared a hall with Carpentry and Home Ec, the smell of sawdust or meatloaf, the whine of a jigsaw or the hum of a blender never penetrated the walls of his sanctuary. All other sensory data was overpowered by the noise of machines engaged in their business. He came to school to listen to it. In time he came to hear the aria of levers and handles and pads, of friction and repetition, at all hours of the day and night. All these machines, he realized one morning on his way to class, would be obsolete almost by the time he graduated from high school. Some of them already were. But the paper slicer was so sharp that even its scissoring was distinguishable in the symphony, and the fact that they were doomed, that somewhere someone was already standing, patent in hand, with the prototype of something that accomplished the same task more efficiently and quicker, was, he realized finally, what sent him soaring. As soon as you learn how to operate me, as soon as you know my ways, I will be gone, sang the dissonant and percussive chorus of this song. Why this brought him such pleasure, when the D he made in the class kept him from an academic scholarship to college, when all the girls and especially the three other boys and even, after his obvious inability to master even the paper cutter with any sort of proficiency, Miss Southerland herself came to ignore him, was the most deliciously unanswerable part of it all.

Sentry

To pay for the trip he had sold an antique derringer that had belonged to his great-grandmother. Also he used up his sick days, which, since he'd gotten sober a year earlier, had been accruing as they did for people not in the habit of passing a hangover off as food poisoning

He was taking his daughter, who had just graduated from college, on a tour of western National Parks, beginning with the Grand Canyon and ending at Yellowstone. They flew into Phoenix, he from Houston, his daughter from Baltimore. Phoenix seemed to him a terrible idea. A desert was lovely and interesting until you paved it and inserted cul-de-sacs and discount shoe outlets. He knew his reaction to be both obvious and true and he entertained it defiantly, as if someone were listening in on his thoughts, about to accuse him of unoriginality. He was especially concerned that his daughter think him original because once, when she was studying in Florence during her junior year abroad, she sent him a letter from Naples, which he still kept, folded, in his wallet.

Today we went to Pompeii which was kind of boring and kind of awesome. I liked the plaster casts of people frozen in terror but then I got worried that that made me a terrible

person. Otherwise I did not really understand the heap of bricks and marble and how exactly the roman baths worked and how they had modern plumbing but still some people in Kentucky and elsewhere do not.

The next morning, as they stood together at the rim of the canyon, he wanted to say that it was kind of boring and kind of awesome, but he worried she might think it weird that these words she wrote to him were what he remembered, out of so many more important words, ones he ought to have written to her? Or better yet, said to her? Yet the Grand Canyon was kind of boring and kind of awesome. Certainly it was vast and deep and there were hawks riding thermals and a great and unsettling silence coming from the majestic and obviously ancient yaw. Still, he was underwhelmed. His daughter's birth had been like that. It did not feel miraculous to him because he had been in the room with her mother for nine hours watching the US Open and occasionally playing games of Spite and Malice, interrupted by her contractions. The moment his daughter emerged and broke into a cry, he faked a sob. He could easily pinpoint that as the beginning of his failure as a parent, but he knew that had his tears been actual, he would have still found his daughter mysterious and often unreachable. Other men had admitted to him that they, too, did not feel instantaneous and undying love for their newborn children, as there seemed nothing much—yet—to love. It slept, shat, screamed, and fed itself into a narcotic stupor at the breast of the woman whose breast was denied you. I didn't really feel anything until it developed a personality, one of his coworkers once told him at happy hour a few weeks after his daughter was born, and when he asked when exactly that occurred, the man had looked away and said, It depends, but I can tell you that this part lasts awhile and you tend to get all up into the smallest things, like, say, when the thing smiles the first time. You have no idea what they're smiling about or what they've got to smile about but of course you go fucking nuts, thinking, Oh man, finally they're having some fun!

They were done with the Grand Canyon by noon. Driving northeast, they entered a Navajo reservation, passing trailers and tiny, tin-roofed houses, clustered in compounds fenced with spindly locust poles and barbed wire, inside of which horses and goats grazed. In the distance, on the broken sandy hills, ATVs cut deep ruts across the desert. He thought of her letter folded in his wallet, wondered if these people, unlike ancient buried-alive Romans, had indoor plumbing. I need a pit stop, said his daughter. He looked down at the map, folded on the console between them. They were somewhere between Tuba City and Tonalea. They drove another five minutes before a store appeared. From a distance it seemed that the place was mobbed, but as it came into view they saw that the store was attached to an abandoned garage, its bay windows broken or boarded up; the vehicles surrounding it were wrecked or wheelless, propped on blocks. Of course not, she said when he asked her if she needed him to come in with her. Alone, he watched a dust devil form in the field across the highway, jump the pavement and settle in the parking lot. His rental car rocked in a gust. Through the brown wind a pickup emerged, coasting past the gas pumps, bumping over the ruts in the lot. A group of young men piled out and filed into the store. Only the last two noticed him and the looks they gave him were somewhere between indifference and contempt. He counted to twenty-five, got out and pushed through the stinging sand. A bell rang above the door as he entered. The trapped odor of fried meat made him breathe through his nose. The woman behind the register looked at him briefly, then went back to talking to another woman, who leaned with both elbows on the counter, as if exhausted or espousing some conspiracy. In back, the boys that had fallen out of the pickup gathered around the pool table and he relaxed at the noise of their laughter and the clack of cue ball breaking a rack.

There was only one bathroom, at the end of a dark hall clogged with boxes. He lingered by the beer coolers, tried not to look at the sweat beading on the bottles. I had to go, too, he would tell his daughter when she emerged, though he had come inside because he did not like the looks of the place. He felt guilty for not liking the looks of this place—he knew if he admitted as much to his daughter, she would think him a bigot—but then something wonderful happened. Suddenly the smell of hot child came over him, along with the feel of the skin— warm and slick with sweat—of his daughter when she was a toddler. Because he had found a buyer for a pistol small enough to fit into a girdle and managed to stay sober long enough to rack up a week of sick leave, he was having, alone, the sort of experience he'd dreamed they'd share at the sight of some tawny western natural wonder.

But it was okay, because he remembered, then, something else he'd forgotten: the way his daughter had stared at the world after awakening from a nap. How she'd studied the trees outside her nursery, first through the bars of a crib and then the crosshatch of window screen, observing, with obvious wonder, the leaves of high trees brushing the afternoon sky. To her there were no obstructions: as far as he knew she was, in her mind, atop the tree, shaking it, stirring up a breeze. He remembered how abandoned he'd felt in those moments, jealous of her interest in the world beyond. How wrong he'd been to make the usual silly noises and faces; any attempt to get her attention in those moments was met with an unnerving glare, as if she saw—even then—through his helpless need to do right by her. He felt as if he was still being viewed through bars and screens and what he had mistaken for his power—his ability to protect and comfort and instruct—was far away and walled off.

In seconds she would open the door to find him there at the top of the dark hallway, standing sentry. He would tell his little lie in the service of love, and he would take his turn in the bathroom, and she would wait for him. Then they would get in the car and drive to the next natural wonder on the list, about which he would try to say something original even though he knew that years from now, when she was his age, maybe with children of her own, all she might remember of this trip was the enormous piece of fry bread she would make him stop for five miles down the road. They would split it, and it would be greasy, and they would not stop talking, even standing in front of Old Faithful, about how awful it was, and how delicious.

Acknowledgments

The Book of Men, edited by Colum McCann	"How to Be a Man"
The Cincinnati Review	"Sunday in the Blue Law Bible Belt"
	"You Can't Talk, Shake a Bush"
Cut Bank	"I Got a Line on You"
Five Points	"Only the Horse Knew the Way"
	"Typingpool"
Inch	"Medicine Girl"
New England Review	"Beamon's Woods" (as "Stop 'N' Go")
The North Carolina Literary Review	"Never Mind"
	"Recruitment"
O Henry Prize Stories: 2014	"Deep Eddy"
The Oxford American	"Concession"
South Carolina Review	"Stragglers"
Southwest Review	"Deep Eddy"
Storysouth	"Ghetto Teacher Film Festival"
Terminus	"Widow's Walk"

"Medicine Girl" is for Jim McHugh.
"Need Not" is for Mark Richard.
"I Got a Line on You" is for Rebecca Bengal.
"Sentry" is for Jesse Donaldson.

The author wishes to thank Ross White, Julia Ridley Smith, and everyone at Bull City Press. Thanks also to Maud Casey, Emma Parker, Terry Kennedy; to Nancy and Nicholas Vacc for their generosity; and to the following bodies of water wherein many of these stories originated: Barton Springs, Deep Eddy, Big Stacy and Mabel Davis public pools in Texas, and the Greensboro Aquatic Center in North Carolina.

About the Author

Michael Parker is the author of six novels—*Hello Down There, Towns Without Rivers, Virginia Lovers, If You Want Me To Stay, The Watery Part of the World,* and *All I Have In This World*—and two collections of stories, *The Geographical Cure* and *Don't Make Me Stop Now.* His fiction and nonfiction have appeared in dozens of journals including *Five Points,* the *Georgia Review, The Idaho Review,* the *Washington Post,* the *New York Times Magazine, Oxford American, Shenandoah, The Black Warrior Review, Trail Runner,* and *Runner's World.* He has received fellowships in fiction from the North Carolina Arts Council and the National Endowment for the Arts, as well as the Hobson Award for Arts and Letters, and the North Carolina Award for Literature. His work has been anthologized in the *Pushcart, New Stories from the South,* and *O. Henry Prize Stories* anthologies. A graduate of the University of North Carolina at Chapel Hill and the University of Virginia, he is the Nicholas and Nancy Vacc Distinguished Professor in the MFA Writing Program at the University of North Carolina at Greensboro.

Also from
Bull City Press